The Bear Under the Stairs

Helen Cooper

For Ted

THE BEAR UNDER THE STAIRS
A PICTURE CORGI BOOK 978 0 552 55845 7

First published in Great Britain by Doubleday,
an imprint of Random House Children's Publishers UK
A Random House Group Company

Doubleday edition published 1993
Picture Corgi edition published 1994
This Picture Corgi edition published 2008

11

Picture Corgi Books are published by Random House Children's Publishers UK
61–63 Uxbridge Road, London W5 5SA

www.randomhousechildrens.co.uk
www.wormworks.com

Addresses for companies within The Random House Group Limited
can be found at: www.randomhouse.co.uk/offices.htm

THE RA███████ ███ ██ Reg. No. 954009

A CIP ███ ███ ████ ███tish Library.

William was scared
of grizzly bears,
and William was scared
of the place
under the stairs.

It was all because
one day he thought
he'd seen a bear, there,
under the stairs.

And he'd **slammed**
the door shut –

WHAM,
BANG,
THUMP!

William worried about the bear.
He wondered what it might eat.
"Yum, yum," the bear said, in William's head.
"I'm a very hungry bear,
perhaps I'll eat boys for tea!"

So William saved a pear
for the bear
who lived under the stairs.

And when no-one was watching,
William whipped out his pear,
opened the door,
threw the pear to the bear
that lived under the stairs,
then **slammed** the door shut –

WHAM,
BANG,
THUMP!

William had kept his eyes shut tight,
so he didn't see the bear
in its lair
under the stairs.

But he knew what it looked like!

And at night . . .

while William dreamed . . .

Every day, William fed
the bear that lived under
the stairs.

He fed it

bananas,

bacon,

and

bread.

He fed it

hazelnuts,

haddock

and honey . . .

But he always kept his eyes
closed tight, and **slammed**
the door shut –
WHAM,
BANG,
THUMP!

After a while there was a strange smell,
in the air,
near the bear,
under the stairs!

The smell got **stronger**, and **stronger**,
until his mum noticed.
"There's an awful pong," she said.
"I think I'd better do some cleaning."

"NO!"

screamed William, very scared.

"DON'T GO in THERE!"

Mum lifted William on to her lap.
"William, whatever's the matter?" she asked.
So William told her all about the hungry bear
in its lair, there, under the stairs.

Then William and Mum went to fight
the bear
that lived under the stairs.
Brave William had his eyes wide open
all the time,
and when they opened the door,
he saw . . .

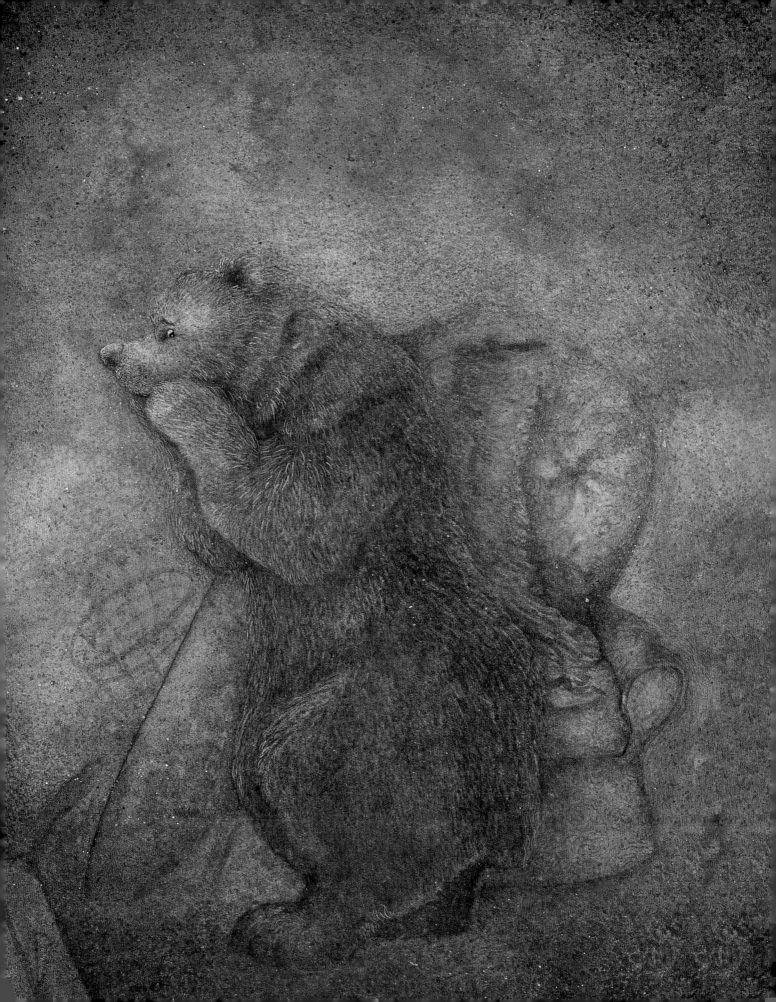

An old furry rug,
a broken chair,
no bear,
no scare,
and horrible stinky food everywhere!

So William and
Mum cleaned up.

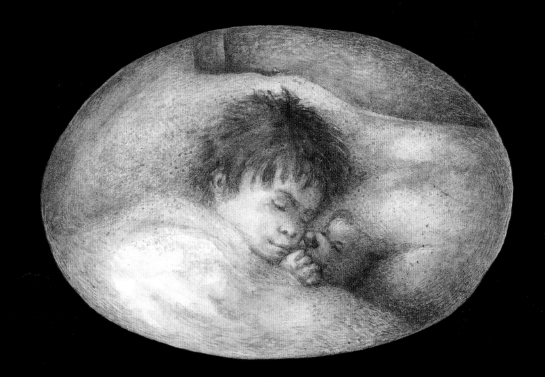

Then they went shopping and
bought William a little brown grizzly
bear of his own. It had such a nice face
that William was never scared of bears . . .

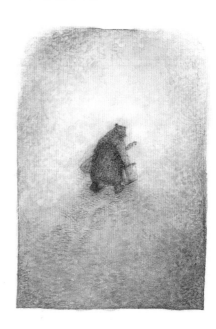

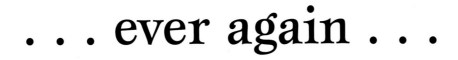

. . . ever again . . .